Lilah

Dyan Sheldon has written several books for children. She and her cats live in London.

Wendy Smith was born in Surrey and studied at the Hornsey and Royal Colleges of Art in London. She has written and illustrated several picture books for children. She and her husband also live in London.

Other books by Dyan Sheldon

A Witch Got On at Paddington Station
(with Wendy Smith)
Harry and Chicken
Harry the Explorer
Seymour Finds a Home
The Whales' Song

Other books by Wendy Smith

Ginger the Whinger
The Lonely Only Mouse
Say Hello, Tilly
Think Hippo!
Twice Mice
The Witch Baby

Dyan Sheldon

Lilah's Monster

Illustrated by Wendy Smith

**YOUNG
PIPER**

Young Piper Original

PAN MACMILLAN
CHILDREN'S BOOKS

First published 1992 by Pan Macmillan Children's Books,
a division of Pan Macmillan Limited
Cavaye Place, London SW10 9PG
9 8 7 6 5 4 3 2 1
Text © Dyan Sheldon 1992
Illustrations © Wendy Smith 1992

ISBN 0 330 32219 2

Printed in England by Clays Ltd, St Ives plc

Monster in the Cupboard

Lilah was perfect.

"You're perfect, Lilah," her parents told her. "You're a perfect little girl."

Lilah wore pretty pink dresses and frilly white socks. She wore a ribbon in her hair and carried a shiny red handbag. She never got mud on her shoes or ketchup down the front of her blouse.

Lilah was always quiet and polite.
She always said "please". "Yes
please," Lilah would say. She always
said "thank you". "No thank you,"
Lilah would reply. She was never
rude or noisy. She never grabbed or
pushed or shoved.

Lilah behaved like a lady. She never ran through the house shouting and screaming. She never chased the cat or tickled the dog. She never stirred the goldfish bowl with a fork. She never ate so many biscuits that she had no room for her dinner. She never gobbled up her food.

"Isn't she just perfect?" Lilah's parents said to one another. "She may not be the most exciting little girl in the world. But she is perfect."

And neat. Lilah was very neat. She
kept her dolls in a row on her bed.
She kept her shoes in a row on her
shoe rack. She kept her books

in a row on her book shelf. Her
games were stacked in a box marked
"toys". Her monster was kept at the
back of her cupboard. Behind the
pink dresses and her navy blue coat.

Lilah's monster was named Annabel. Annabel was small and furry. She was green with purple polka dots and enormous orange eyes.

In the morning, when Lilah was
cheerfully getting ready for school,
Annabel snuggled up on a pile of
old blankets on the floor of the
cupboard.

All day long, while Lilah was at school, being perfect, Annabel slept.

In the afternoon, while Lilah sat at her desk, happily doing her homework, Annabel snored.

While Lilah was smilingly helping to lay the table for tea, Annabel dreamed.

At about the time that Lilah, more
perfect than ever, was washing her
face and brushing her teeth and
putting on her nightdress, Annabel
was rolling over and rubbing her
eyes.

Every night, Lilah's mother tucked Lilah into bed. "Good-night, sweetheart," whispered Lilah's mother. She kissed Lilah on the cheek.

"Good-night, Mother dear," Lilah whispered back.

"Sleep tight," sang Lilah's mother. "Don't let the bed bugs bite."

"Oh, I won't," said Lilah. "You know I won't."

It was after Lilah's parents had turned off all the lights and gone to bed and the house was still that Annabel usually woke up. She yawned. She stretched. She rubbed her eyelids. She opened the cupboard door with a bang.

In the darkness of Lilah's room, all that could be seen were Annabel's enormous orange eyes.

Annabel was a perfect monster.
Annabel was always a mess. Her
hair was never combed. Her ribbon
was always undone.

Her shoes were never buckled. Her
socks were always clumped around
her ankles. There were always bits
of chocolate stuck in her fur.

Annabel was never quiet.
She growled. She farted. She burped.

"Shush, Annabel," Lilah would
warn her. "You'll wake everyone
up."

Annabel didn't care. She lumbered around the room, knocking things over. Lilah put them right. She undressed Lilah's dolls and stood them on their heads. Lilah put their clothes back on them and sat them on their bottoms.

She took the dress that Lilah had laid out for the next day and threw it on the floor. Lilah hung it up again. She dumped all the games in Lilah's toy box on the rug. "Oh, Annabel," sighed Lilah, as she picked them up again. "Just look at the mess you've made."

But Annabel didn't care about that
either. Every night she took the glass
of water Lilah's mother always left
on the bedside table and threw it
over Lilah.

"Wake up, Lilah!" Annabel
roared. "Wake up! I'm bored." She
shook Lilah's shoulder. "Come on,"
she shouted. "Let's have some fun!"

Lilah's idea of fun was to brush her dolls' hair, or to play with a puzzle, or to read a book. But Annabel had a monstrous idea of fun.

Annabel made Lilah ride down the banister.

"Bombs away!" Annabel yelled.

"Bombs away!" shrieked Lilah.

She made Lilah jump on the
furniture. They jumped on the sofa,

and then they jumped on the chairs.
"Higher!" Annabel screamed
breathlessly. "You have to jump
higher than that!"

"You mean like this?" Lilah
screamed back, bumping her head
on the ceiling.

Annabel loved pillow fights.

"Nah, nah," Annabel teased, ducking behind a chest of drawers. "You can't hit me!"

Lilah thumped Annabel with one of the cushions from the sofa.

"You mean like this?" she'd shout.
"No, like this," giggled Annabel,
whopping her back.

Annabel liked to play with the cat. She and Lilah snuck up behind the sleeping cat, very very quietly. "Boo!" they shouted into the cat's ear. Laughing, they fell into each other's arms as the cat raced from the room. "Did you see her face?" they'd gasp. "Did you see the way she ran?"

Annabel and Lilah sat on the dog.
"Giddy-up," they laughed.
"Giddy-up, little doggy!" They
laughed even harder when
the dog hid under the
table.
"Where are you going?" they'd
scream. "Don't you want
to play?"

Sometimes Annabel liked to play hide and seek. Lilah was always it. She tiptoed through the house, calling, "Annabel! Annabel! Where are you?"

Annabel always had great hiding places. She hid in the light over the dining room table. She hid in the pantry. She hid in the broom cupboard. She'd suddenly jump out of the laundry basket, rolling her eyes.

Annabel always liked to eat. She and Lilah raided the refrigerator. They ate cold spaghetti. They ate pickles from the jar. They finished off the cake. They drank the juice from the container.

They climbed up onto the kitchen
cupboard and ate all the biscuits.

"Isn't this fun?" Annabel laughed.
"Isn't this fun?" laughed Lilah.

But as soon as the night started to
slip away and the sky began to
brighten, Annabel became tired.

Annabel yawned. Annabel rubbed her big orange eyes. "Time for bed," said Annabel sleepily. "I've got to get my beauty sleep."

Lilah slipped back between her covers. Annabel went back into the cupboard.

In the morning, Lilah's mother came into her room to wake her up. "I don't know what I'm going to do about that dog and that cat," she said, shaking her head. "They run about making a mess all night long." She drew back the curtains. She smiled. "Did you have a good dream, darling?" asked Lilah's mother.

Lilah rolled over. Lilah stretched.
Lilah yawned. "Oh, yes," said Lilah.
"I had a perfect dream."

"Of course you did," said Lilah's
mother. "You're such a perfect
little girl."

Monster out of the Cupboard

Lilah went off to school in her neat pink dress and her long white socks and her shiny black shoes. She carried her lunch in a pink plastic box. There were pretty pink bows in her hair. Lilah's mother waved her good-bye from the front door. "Good-bye, darling," called Lilah's mother. "Be good." And then she laughed to herself. Of course Lilah would be good. Lilah was always good. In fact, she was perfect.

While Lilah was at school, Lilah's mother tidied up the house.

"There's a place for everything," Lilah's mother always said. "And everything in its place."

Lilah's mother tidied up the living room. Lilah's mother tidied up the kitchen. Lilah's mother put everything in the bathroom away. Lilah's mother went into Lilah's room. Naturally, everything in Lilah's room was already in its place.

"How nice to have such a perfect little girl," said Lilah's mother, with a happy smile. She blew a piece of fluff off the lampshade. She sat one of Lilah's dolls a little straighter on the bed.

She opened the door to the cupboard.

"Oh, my goodness," said Lilah's mother. "What's this?" There was something on the floor of Lilah's cupboard. Lilah's mother frowned. She shook her head. "There shouldn't be anything on the floor of Lilah's cupboard," said Lilah's mother. She peered in. There seemed to be a pile of old blankets on the floor. Old blankets and something furry, green and covered with bright purple dots.

She kicked it with her toe.

"Is that the rug that used to be in the hall?" asked Lilah's mother. But the furry green thing with the bright purple dots was not the rug that used to be in the hall. It was Lilah's monster, Annabel. Annabel opened her gigantic orange eyes.

"Agghhhh!" screamed Lilah's mother. Lilah's mother had not been expecting eyes.

"Agghhhh!" screamed Annabel.
Annabel had not been expecting
Lilah's mother.

Not too far from Lilah's house, the school bell rang and the doors opened. The girls came out together in noisy groups. They were laughing and shouting. They were running and jumping. They were shoving each other and linking arms. Except for Lilah.

Lilah came out of school by herself.
She walked slowly and kept her eyes
on the ground.

The other girls teased her.

"Ooh, Lilah," they giggled, "what are you going to do this afternoon, brush your teeth?"

"What do you do for fun, Lilah?" they yelled after her. "Comb your hair?"

They followed her down the path.
  "Lilah's so boring she bores
herself!" they roared. This made
them giggle even more.

Lilah bit her lip. And then Lilah saw
her, waiting at the entrance. A
sudden smile lit up Lilah's face.

Lilah had not been expecting Annabel.

"Annabel!" cried Lilah. "Annabel, what are you doing here?"

Annabel was swinging on the gate.
She was wearing a mucky-looking
school uniform over her furry green
and purple body. She was chewing
gum and blowing bubbles. She was
kicking stones into the road. Her
shoes were filthy. There was
strawberry jam on her chin. She
looked cross.

The other girls came to a halt
behind Lilah. They stopped giggling.
They stopped shouting.

"Who is that?" they asked each
other. "She can't be a friend of Lilah's."

Annabel wiped her nose on her
sleeve.

"I've just had the fright of my
life," said Annabel. She stood on her
head. "And now I want to have some
fun."

The other girls couldn't believe their
ears.

"Fun?" they shouted. "Fun with
Lilah? Nobody has fun with Lilah.
She's too perfect."

Annabel stuck out her tongue at
them.

"I'm not talking to you," said
Annabel. "So shut up."

"Well I don't know," said Lilah in
a whisper. She glanced at the other
girls. She glanced at her watch. "My
parents ... I really should get
home..."

"We're going home," said
Annabel. She grinned. "But we can
have some fun on the way." She did
a cartwheel. Then she did another.

"Annabel!" gasped Lilah. But she was already forgetting about her parents and the tea that would be served at precisely five-thirty. She was already forgetting about the other girls. She grinned back at Annabel. "You can't do cartwheels in the street in broad daylight."

Annabel did another cartwheel. "Oh yes I can," said Annabel with a wink. Then she gave Lilah a sly look. "Bet you can't," she said.

"Of course I can," said Lilah.

"Bet you can't."

Lilah did a cartwheel.

"Bet you can't do as many as I can do," shouted Annabel.

Lilah and Annabel cartwheeled
out of the school entrance. They
cartwheeled down the street.

The other girls ran behind them.
    "Hey! Wait for us!" they cried.
"Wait for us!"

Annabel landed in a puddle
with a big splash. "This is what
puddles are for!" she laughed.
"This is what I call fun!"
   "Me, too!" laughed Lilah.
   "Us, too!" laughed the other girls.

Lilah started hopping through the puddle on one leg. "Follow the leader!" she shouted. "Follow me!"

Annabel started hopping on one leg.
The other girls followed. Shouting
and giggling, they all hopped
through the puddle.

"Follow the leader!" cried Annabel. She started swinging from the trees. "Follow me!"

The other girls started swinging
from the trees. But none of them
could swing as fast or as high as
Lilah. None of the others could quite
keep up with Annabel. "Hey, wait
for us!" they called. "Lilah! Annabel!
Wait for us!"

Lilah led them to the park. They
hung from the parallel bars by
their knees. They swung through
the air on a thick piece of rope

screaming, "Yaaaaaaaaaaa!"
They ran along the lakeside,
quacking like ducks.

"We never guessed you knew
someone like Annabel," the other
girls said to Lilah. "We never knew
you could be so much fun."

Lilah was smiling and blushing with pleasure. But then a thought occurred to her. The thought that occurred to Lilah was Lilah's mother and father. The smile froze on her face. She looked at her watch. "Oh, no!" wailed Lilah. "We'll never get home in time for tea!"

"Of course we will," snapped Annabel. "Won't we, girls?"

"Of course we will," cried the other girls.

"Race you!" shouted Annabel.

"Race you!" shouted the other girls.

And they lifted Lilah onto their shoulders and started running through the park. Through the park and out onto the street and down the hill towards Lilah's home, just in time for tea.

Lilah's father kissed her good-night
before she went upstairs. Lilah's
mother tucked her into bed. "Good-
night, darling," said Lilah's mother.
She gave her a peck on the cheek.
"Sweet dreams."

"Good-night, Mother dear," said
Lilah.

Lilah's mother checked that the curtains were drawn. She smoothed down the duvet. She opened the door to the cupboard. "You won't forget what I said about leaving old blankets on the floor, will you, Lilah?" asked Lilah's mother. "I can't tell you how much it upset me."

"Of course I'll remember, Mother dear," said Lilah sleepily.

Lilah's mother poked her head into
the cupboard. The floor was clear.
She gave a contented sigh.

"After all," said Lilah's mother,
"everything has its place."

"And everything in its place,"
said Lilah.

On the top shelf of the cupboard,
behind the box that held Lilah's ice
skates, Annabel opened her
enormous orange eyes.

All Pan books are available at your local bookshop or newsagent, or can be ordered direct from the publisher. Indicate the number of copies required and fill in the form below.

Send to: **CS Department, Pan Books Ltd., P.O. Box 40, Basingstoke, Hants. RG21 2YT.**

or phone: 0256 469551 (Ansaphone), quoting title, author and Credit Card number.

Please enclose a remittance* to the value of the cover price plus: 60p for the first book plus 30p per copy for each additional book ordered to a maximum charge of £2.40 to cover postage and packing.

*Payment may be made in sterling by UK personal cheque, postal order, sterling draft or international money order, made payable to Pan Books Ltd.

Alternatively by Barclaycard/Access:

Card No.																		

Signature:

Applicable only in the UK and Republic of Ireland.

While every effort is made to keep prices low, it is sometimes necessary to increase prices at short notice. Pan Books reserve the right to show on covers and charge new retail prices which may differ from those advertised in the text or elsewhere.

NAME AND ADDRESS IN BLOCK LETTERS PLEASE:

....

Name ————————————————————————————

Address ————————————————————————————

————————————————————————————————

————————————————————————————————

————————————————————————————————

3/87